I hope you enjoy the book.
Happy reading!
Love-
Aunt Hope

We would like to thank all our supporters, both big and small, who have made this book a reality. Special thanks to our business supporters: Shan How Realtor, Matzinger-Davies Wine, Hopscotch Toys, and Daily Driven Motors. We would also like to thank Tony Lai and Logan Schobel for helping to make the book better. Lastly, thanks to all of you who are supporting children who are going through trauma, and rescue organizations that are doing the same for animals.

www.mascotbooks.com

THE TRIUMPHANT TAILS OF RESCUE DOGS: PUNK'S PLIGHT

For more information, please contact:
Mascot Books
620 Herndon Parkway, Suite 320
Herndon, VA 20170
info@mascotbooks.com

Library of Congress Control Number: 2020925811

CPSIA Code: PRT0321A

ISBN-13: 978-1-64543-926-4

Printed in the United States

THE TRIUMPHANT TAILS OF RESCUE DOGS
PUNK'S PLIGHT

Written by Hope A. Walter, EdD

Illustrated by Susi B. Davis

DEDICATION

This is the story of Pumpkin the bulldog. A
few names and places have been changed.
Thank you to Pacific Northwest Bulldog
Rescue Shelter for saving Pumpkin. I do not
know what I would have done without her.

They call me Punky, Pumpkin Pie, Punky-Doo, and Pumpkin, but you can call me Punk. I know what you're thinking. You think I have an easy, carefree life. And you are right. My life's great now, but it wasn't always this way.

When I was born, I was adopted by a family who really wanted an English Bulldog (that's me). They named me Pumpkin, and not to brag, but I was so cute. Everyone loved me, and I was happy. But as I got older, my family had less time for me. They stopped taking care of me. I felt like they had forgotten about me.

I was still the same lovable and cute pup, but they no longer paid attention to me. If I wanted to go outside or wanted attention, they got mad at me, even though I didn't do anything wrong. They told me I was a pest. No one cared about me or my needs. Feeling like I didn't matter made me very sad.

Unfortunately, that's not all. My skin became itchy and infected. And my hair fell out! I am not sure if you noticed, but I don't have a normal tail, and it gets stinky if it is not taken care of properly. So I stank, I lost my hair, and I didn't look very cute anymore. I had given up. I had lost hope.

One day when I was out in my yard, a man walked by and noticed that I was not looking healthy. He asked my family if he could help me . . . and they said yes! I knew my family couldn't afford the care I needed, but I felt sick and like they were throwing me away. I didn't know this man. Could I trust him? But I left anyway. What choice did I have?!

We arrived at a giant farmhouse with the words "Rescue and Recovery Ranch" written on a big, red barn. Xavier (the man who found me) ran the rescue ranch for neglected and abused animals. He told me neglect is when someone is mistreated or not taken care of properly. Xavier said all the animals at the rescue were here to recover from abuse or neglect. For the first time, I understood that there were others just like me.

When I first arrived, I was not sure if I could trust anyone. I stayed in my bed, slept a lot, and felt too terrible to eat. The Rescue and Recovery crew gave me a check-up to see how they could help me. They explained everything and asked my permission before they touched me. I liked that. It made me feel like I was in control. They gave me medicine for my skin, a bath to help my tail, and a soft place to lay my head. This made me feel like they cared.

At first, I stayed away from everyone. I didn't want to risk getting hurt again. As I watched the other animals talking and playing with Xavier and each other, I felt alone. I tried to go out into the rescue center, but I got too scared. Eventually, I was brave enough to join them, and I felt relieved when I was not alone anymore.

I started to spend more time with Xavier and the other dogs. Xavier told us stories about dogs who had recovered at the ranch. He said the rescue ranch found good families for some of the dogs. He made it sound great, but it really frightened me to think about going anywhere else.

Slowly, my body began to heal. My stinky tail felt much better, my skin was no longer cracked, and my fur even began to grow back! Although I was looking and feeling better, there were still wounds inside my heart that needed to heal. I still felt scared and alone.

One day, Xavier let me ride with him on his rescue missions. I love car rides! Xavier said he understood how I felt. When he was a boy, his parents could not take care of him, so he was sent to foster care. Xavier moved from foster home to foster home. He said he never felt like he had a home of his own. When he grew up, he started the Rescue and Recovery Ranch to help others find forever homes, since he never had one himself.

I felt like Xavier understood me, and I felt safe for the first time in a very long time. But it made me confused, too. Although I felt happy at the ranch, I still missed my old home and my family. I still loved them, even after they mistreated me. It was hard to have so many different feelings all at once.

After a few months at the shelter, Xavier said he found a family that wanted to adopt me. I was so scared! I had a family before, and they had stopped taking care of me. Why should I trust this new family? I wanted to stay at the ranch with Xavier, but he told me his job was to help me become a "triumphant tail" (as he called them). I knew he was trying to help me. I hoped he was right.

Xavier drove me to meet my new family. When I met my new parents, they talked softly and calmly to me and held out their hands for me to sniff. I was too scared to move. Xavier packed up my things and told me he loved me. It felt wonderful to hear that, but I was sad to be losing Xavier. I was so confused, and there was nothing I could do about it. It was hard to feel helpless.

Suddenly, I was on my way to Oregon with my new family. My new mom told me that I was safe and that they would take good care of me. She said it was okay to be scared. She sat close to me, but stayed far enough to give me my space. It was like she understood what I needed.

When we arrived at my new home, everyone was already asleep. I was relieved because I was too afraid to meet anyone else that night. The other pets in the house came to sniff me, but I just hid in my bed. I had too many feelings in my heart and head. I just needed to be alone.

The next day, I heard lots of little feet and excited voices. As I met the boys, my new mom reminded them to be calm and patient with me until I learned to trust them. They approached me quietly, held out their hands, and waited for me. They would come lay beside me. Everyone wanted to be with me. I felt like a celebrity. It felt nice to be wanted.

But, moving to another home and a new family was hard for me. Everything was different. I missed Xavier and the ranch. I missed my first family and home. I wanted to be where things were the same, but now I was in a new house with new people. It made my brain and body so tired.

Learning a new life took time. Each day I slowly felt more comfortable. The house was busy and noisy, but the family was patient with me. Even little noises made me run and hide. My mom told me it was normal to be scared, and she told me to come out when *I* was ready. This made me feel powerful and in control for once.

I started to feel like I found my forever family. I felt safe when I was around them. They even started to call me Punk, which is short for Pumpkin. I liked it. It made me sound tough. Sometimes I barked at people when they came to my house. I wanted them to think that I was brave and strong. They were in *my* house now.

My family taught other people to wait for me and that I'd come to them when I was ready. Seeing people wait for me made me relax. It made me feel brave enough to come up to them and get to know them. I felt proud of the steps I was taking to get better. I never forgot how it felt to be mistreated, but I felt stronger and happier than before.

It is hard to trust people once you have been neglected. Even now, eight years later, I still get scared around new people. My mom told me it is normal to feel this way. So, I keep trying. It takes a lot of courage to try to trust again. I am proud of all the work I have done. It takes time and a lot of patience to learn to trust again, but if I can do it, you can, too.

My days are now filled with morning car rides (my favorite) and sleeping next to one of my boys. I stick out my tongue and snore loudly in their ears. I love to rest my head on their arms or backs. My mom says I am the best pup in the world. I think she is probably right.

This is my story of neglect. I have been forever changed, but I am not forever damaged.[1] Healing takes time. Some of my fur will never grow back, and I am still uncomfortable around new people. But I've gotten so much better. I could not have done it without Xavier, my Rescue Ranch friends, or my family, who made me feel safe, included me, and took such good care of me. But, mostly, I know now that I was the one who worked the hardest to learn to love and trust again. I've become stronger and healthier.

If you or someone you know are being mistreated, ask for help from a trusted adult. You can do it, just like I did. As for me, it's time for my daily car ride. If you see me around, remember, take your time with me. I might be the best pup in the world, but I am still fragile on the inside.

Do you think you are being neglected or know someone who is being neglected?

Do you feel alone and scared? Are you afraid to trust the adults around you? If so, here's what Punk says to do.

1. TELL SOMEONE YOU TRUST.

If you are feeling like no one cares about you or you are not being taken care of (food, warmth, clothing, love, and safety), tell your teacher or an adult who listens to you and makes you feel comfortable and safe. Ask for help. I know that is hard, but you must be brave and ask for help. If the first adult you find cannot help, ask another trusted adult. There are adults who *will* help you.

2. REMEMBER IT IS NOT YOUR FAULT.

Remember that even if bad things happen to you, you are not bad. Bad things happened to me, but they were not my fault. You are not alone, and there are good people around who will help you.

3. KNOW YOU ARE NOT DAMAGED.

Being mistreated does not have to damage you forever. You can get help. You can feel better, and people will help you just like they helped me. You deserve to feel safe, happy, and loved.

4. BE A HERO!

I would not be here today if Xavier did not step in to help me. He is my hero, and you can be a hero, too! If you see someone who is sad, hurting, or scared, help them! People who are hurting feel bad about themselves. Sometimes people who are being neglected pretend to act tough when they are being treated badly. They feel like no one cares what happens to them. Be there for them, listen to them, and tell them to talk to someone. A trusted adult can help them get the help that they need.

A Resource for Adults
HOW TO CREATE POSITIVE CHILDHOOD EXPERIENCES (PCE)

Four main areas help foster positive childhood
experiences to create mentally healthy adults:[2]

1. CREATE NURTURING AND SUPPORTIVE RELATIONSHIPS

Children need to feel secure to form healthy relationships with adults. It is recommended children have at least two healthy, safe, non-parent adult relationships (such as teachers, coaches, or counselors) to create PCEs. These relationships need to be responsive, be sustainable, and provide a feeling of safety and trust for the children.

2. PROVIDE SAFE, STABLE, AND EQUITABLE LEARNING ENVIRONMENTS

Learning environments that are safe, stable, and equitable to all children allow them to learn, play, and develop. Physical activity, quality learning opportunities, and access to food, shelter, and medical care are necessary. Consistency allows students to feel safe and protected.

3. PROVIDE OPPORTUNITIES TO ENGAGE SOCIALLY AND DEVELOP A SENSE OF CONNECTEDNESS

Children need to feel a sense of belonging with friends, family, and within the school or classroom. They need to feel respect for their culture and believe they are valued in order to develop a sense of connectedness.

4. TEACH SOCIO-EMOTIONAL COMPETENCY

It is important to teach children how to express feelings in socially appropriate ways. They need adults who are supportive and can help them talk about their feelings, help them regulate their own behavior, and learn how to problem-solve and communicate effectively with others.

ABOUT THE AUTHOR

Hope A. Walter, EdD grew up in East Greenville, Pennsylvania. After graduating from Upper Perkiomen High School, Hope received her BS in Elementary Education at Kutztown University in 1996, her MS in Educational Psychology in 2002 from the University of Las Vegas in Nevada, and her EdD in Educational Leadership in 2018. Currently, Hope resides in McMinnville, Oregon with her husband of twenty-five years, her three boys, and her two dogs and two cats. She works as an adjunct professor at Linfield University and Oregon State University teaching mathematics education and educational psychology to future teachers.

Punk's Plight was conceptualized after teaching future teachers about Adverse Childhood Experiences (ACEs). Hope saw the connection between ACEs and the journey of her own bulldog, Pumpkin, who was neglected, rescued, and spent the rest of her life learning how to trust and love again. Sadly, Pumpkin passed away peacefully in November 2020 after a long life with the Walter family. Hope wants Punk's story to help children suffering from neglect by showing children they can recover, heal, and prosper despite experiencing neglect.

ABOUT THE ILLUSTRATOR

Susi B. Davis has been painting and creating her whole life. She received her BFA from the University of Georgia and followed a creative career first as a graphic artist, then as a fine artist, painting and teaching. She fell in love with watercolors in high school and still prefers that medium.

From a young age, Susi always had a great connection with animals, having raised turtles, rabbits, horses, and, of course, dogs. She is very fortunate to be able to use her love for both watercolor and animals to paint portraits and to spread creativity through art classes for all ages in parks, homes, and retirement centers.

She lives in Oregon and is married with three nearly grown, creative children and two dogs, presently. When she is not painting, Susi can be found running, biking, skiing, or hiking.